George Most Wanted

Ingrid Lee

with illustrations by Stéphane Denis

ORCA BOOK PUBLISHERS

National Library of Canada Cataloguing in Publication Data

Lee, Ingrid, 1948-
George most wanted / Ingrid Lee;
with illustrations by Stéphane Denis.
(Orca echoes)

ISBN 1-55143-472-5

I. Denis, Stéphane, 1971- II. Title. III. Series.

PS8623.E44G46 2005   jC813'.6   C2005-904060-2

First Published in the United States: 2005
Library of Congress Control Number: 2005929687

Summary: George is a small plastic toy who went for a ride on a rocket and flew apart. Now all his parts must find each other.

Orca Book Publishers gratefully acknowledges the support for its publishing programs provided by the following agencies: the Government of Canada through the Department of Canadian Heritage's Book Publishing Industry Development Program (BPIDP), the Canada Council for the Arts, and the British Columbia Arts Council.

Design and typesetting by Lynn O'Rourke

Orca Book Publishers   Orca Book Publishers
PO Box 5626, Stn. B   PO Box 468
Victoria, BC Canada   Custer, WA USA
V8R 6S4   98240-0468

www.orcabook.com
Printed and bound in Canada
Printed on 50% post-consumer recycled paper,
processed chlorine free using vegetable, low VOC inks.

08 07 06 05 • 4 3 2 1

To Johnny and Daniel.

Before the Story Begins

George was a little guy made out of plastic. He had pink skin and black hair. He always wore a red jumpsuit and shiny red shoes.

Katie and Mackenzie tied George to a dragon rocket on fireworks day. Their mother set off the rocket. She did not see the plastic guy tied to the side. So up he went!

The air got colder and colder. The jets got hotter and hotter.
Boom!

Ten thousand lights exploded around him.

Boom! Boom! Boom!

George couldn't decide what to do. One arm wanted to go one way. The other arm wanted to go another way. And the legs wouldn't follow each other.

It was every part for itself!

George's parts went everywhere. All Katie and Mackenzie could find were a leg and a shoe.

Will George ever get back together again?

George
Lands on a Blackberry

George fell through blackberry space. He was out of control! He chipped the point off a star. He sliced the tail off a comet. He diced some moonbeams.

Chop, chop! Bits of the night flew everywhere.

George tried to steer the rocket, but he had no hands. How could he steer the rocket without his big strong hands?

He stepped on the brakes, but he had no shoes. How could he stop the rocket without his shiny red shoes?

George looked down. His jumpsuit was gone. His body was gone. And so was his rocket. All he saw was a big dark planet. He was going to crash!

George kept his head. He was not going to smack his face. He would land lightly!

George shook all the heavy thoughts out of his head. He forgot about elephants and bowling balls. He forgot about schoolbags. He filled his thoughts with clouds and cotton candy.

Ploomph!

George fell into a purple pillow. It tasted sweet—as sweet as blackberry juice.

Mmmm! George sank into the purple pillow. He would have a blackberry soda. He would have a nap. Then he would find his missing parts.

He was George the Brave, George the Steadfast. He still had his big blue eyes and his long straight nose. He still had the waves in his hair.

He had a good head start!

George
Gets In a Jam

A dad and his little boy went blackberry picking. "Put ten berries in the basket," said Mr. Mohan to his little boy. "Then put one in the mouth. That's the picking rule."

The little boy began to pick berries. He didn't see the plastic head lying on the ground. Why would he? The head sat in the middle of a blackberry. The head was covered with purple juice. The head looked more like a blackberry than the blackberry.

The little boy picked it up and popped it…in the basket! It was only number ten.

At home, his daddy threw the berries in a bag. He didn't see George's head, but he felt it. "Some of these berries are still a bit hard," he said. He opened the door of the freezer and stuck the bag inside.

The little boy asked, "Why can't we eat the berries now?"

"You had lots," said his father. He shut the freezer door. "We'll keep those ones for later."

"Our berries are the best of all!" the little boy said.

Katie and Mackenzie Make Posters

The morning after fireworks day, Katie and Mackenzie went out to the backyard. They looked around for the rest of George. There was nothing there.

"All we have is a left leg and a shoe," Mackenzie said. "We should make missing posters."

Katie had nothing better to do. She said okay.

Mackenzie got out his crayons. He had twenty-four colors. "I'll make the pictures," he said.

He drew George. He colored the hair black and the jumpsuit red. He made the shoes red too. The skin was pink.

"He has blue eyes," said Katie.

"I was just going to do that," Mackenzie said. He took a blue crayon and colored the circles blue.

Mackenzie made three pictures. Each drawing was a little different.

In the first drawing, George was too good-looking. "He doesn't look like that," said Katie. "His pants are too tight. He's not a rock star."

The last drawing was the easiest. Mackenzie drew the back of the little guy. He drew George's black hair, his red back, his red legs and his little red bum.

The second drawing was the best. George had just the right shape. His eyes were just the right size.

After Mackenzie finished each picture, Katie wrote the words.

Mackenzie said, "Don't forget to write *Reward*. You can't ask people to look for nothing."

"I was just going to do that," Katie said. She stuck the word *Reward* into every poster.

"If somebody finds a part, you can give them one of your mutant mud rats," Katie said to her brother. "Or you can give away your Most-Amazing-Wrestler cards."

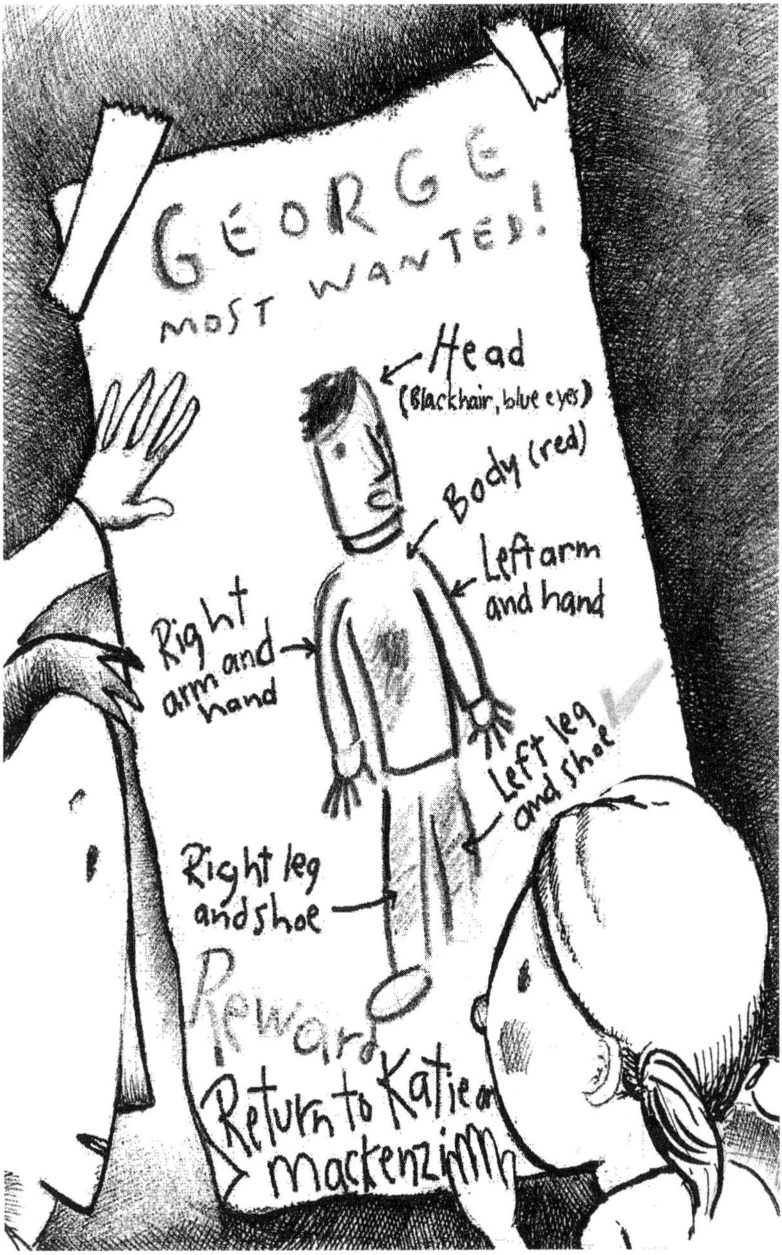
GEORGE
MOST WANTED!
Head
(Black hair, blue eyes)
Body (red)
Left arm and hand
Right arm and hand
Left leg and shoe
Right leg and shoe
Reward
Return to Katie and Mackenzie

Mackenzie looked at Katie as if she had two heads. He looked at her as if she were a mud rat. "No way!" he said. "You can give away your gel pens. Or you can give away your glow-in-the-dark stars."

After that they didn't talk about the reward.

They put the poster with the good-looking George in the grocery store at the corner. They taped the best poster on a pickup truck parked in a driveway down the street.

"The last poster can go here," Katie said. She stuck the picture of George's backside on their front door.

George looked like he was walking into the house.

George's Arm
Falls Down a Chimney

A plastic arm and hand flew through the dark night. It was a left arm. The hand was left too. They went up high. The hand almost poked the moon in the eye.

They began to fall.

Bink!

The arm and the hand fell down a chimney! On the way down the air got hotter and hotter. It got as hot as a pot on the stove. It got as hot as the temper in a tantrum. It got hotter than a spoonful of red pepper sauce.

The arm and the hand landed in a pile of ashes. The ashes were still hot. One of the glowing coals toasted the plastic parts.

The thumb melted a little bit.

Slowly the fire went out. The arm sank deeper and deeper into the ash. The little pink hand made an angel in the dust.

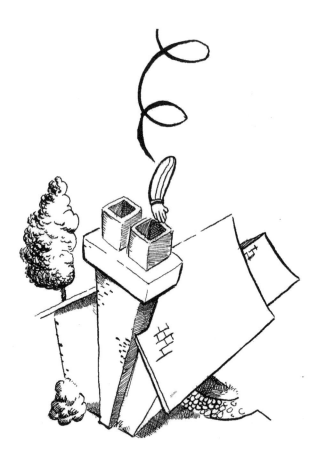

Mackenzie
Finds George's Arm

On the weekend, an old man opened his fireplace. He shoveled the ashes into a pail. He carried the pail outside. The ashes were for his garden. The old man used a rake to spread them around his roses.

The little red arm and the pink hand got stuck between the long teeth of the rake. That put the old man in a grumpy mood.

"What's this?" he grumbled. He shook the rake. The arm and the hand stayed stuck. The old man pulled them loose with his fingers.

He lifted them up to have a look.

That was funny. It looked as if the old man and George's arm were shaking hands.

"This looks like a piece of junk from the kids next door," the old man said. "Those kids should keep their stuff in their own backyard. People shouldn't bother an old man like me." He tossed the arm and the hand over the fence.

Mackenzie was watching the ants under the kitchen window.

Bonk!

The piece of plastic hit his head. It bounced off and landed on the grass. Mackenzie stared at the little red arm. He stared at the little pink hand. He called his sister. Katie stuck her head out the window.

Mackenzie pointed to the arm and the hand. "It fell out of the sky," he said. "Just now."

Katie just shook her head. "You better come in before something else falls down," she said.

Mackenzie picked up the arm and the hand. He went around to the front door and scratched out the words *Left arm and hand* on the poster. He counted the other parts.

Four pieces were still missing.

George's Leg Gets Hooked

A plastic leg hopped down the hill. A red shoe went too. They didn't look where they were going. You need a head for that.

They flipped into a river. The water smelled worse than cheese breath, worse than old shoes. That didn't bother the leg and the shoe. Legs and shoes don't have noses. The leg and the shoe sank.

A catfish watched from the river bottom. It was a big old fish with a wide flat nose and a horseshoe mouth. It even had whiskers.

The catfish was always watching out for something to eat. After dinner it watched for breakfast. After breakfast it watched for lunch. Then it watched for dinner.

That old fish had seen minnows and pollies, duck bottoms and daisy petals, rubber boots and dirty feet. But it had never seen a bright red leg with a shiny red shoe.

Snack time!

The fish opened its great big mouth.

Chomp!

All that fish got was a drink of river. A silver hook stole the leg and the shoe right out of the fish's mouth.

It was a miracle!

Katie and Mackenzie Get George's Leg

The fisherman reeled in his fishing line. He looked at the plastic piece stuck to his silver hook.

"Hmmph!" he snorted. "That's not a fish. That's just a piece of plastic."

"You hooked a leg," said his granddaughter. "You got a shoe too. I saw a poster in the grocery store. People are looking for those two."

She stuck the plastic piece in her pocket.

Later the girl went to Katie and Mackenzie's. She knocked on the door. George's picture was stuck on the door. The girl gave his backside a good whacking.

Katie and Mackenzie answered.

"Here's your leg," the girl said. "It still has the shoe."

"Thanks," said Katie and Mackenzie. They shut the door.

There was another knock at the door. When they opened it again, the girl was still there. "Isn't there a reward?" she asked.

Katie looked at her brother. He looked at his feet. Katie went up to her room. She came back with an oyster shell from the Chinese buffet. "Here," she said.

"Nice reward," said the girl.

After the girl left, Mackenzie crossed out the words *Right leg and shoe* on the poster on the front door. He counted the other parts.

Three pieces were still missing.

Katie and Mackenzie Get Some Parts

A few days later, Mackenzie went to the front door to get the mail.

Clunk!

Something fell through the letter slot. It was a red cape made out of plastic. Maybe it was a superhero cape. Maybe it belonged to Red Riding Hood. Lots of little figures have red capes.

"Hey!" Mackenzie said. "This part doesn't belong to George. George can't fly."

Katie came out of the kitchen. "What?' she asked.

The letter slot opened again.

Clunk!

A tiny blue helmet rolled across the floor.

Katie and Mackenzie stared at it. The letter slot opened again.

Clunk! Clunk! Clunk!

Clang!

Things kept coming through the door. After a bit there was a pile of plastic parts on the floor. There was a curly wig, a black mask, a webbed foot, three buttons and a first-prize ribbon. Everything made a noise but the ribbon. Ribbons are quiet.

Most of the pieces were red. But someone put a little green purse through the mail slot. Some people see green and think red.

Katie and Mackenzie put all the parts in a box. None of the pieces belonged to George. One of them was a lizard tail. What kind of little guy has a tail like a lizard? Maybe some people didn't look at the posters carefully. Some people can't even see the nose on their face.

"Maybe someone will drop off a pair of goggles," said Mackenzie. "George would look good in goggles."

"He'd look better with a head," said Katie.

All day long, things fell into the box. A green motor-cycle made the biggest clunk. It had three wide tires with chrome spokes, a black leather seat and red flames shooting along the sides.

"Wow!" said Mackenzie

"Nobody knows what they're doing," said Katie.

A Newspaper
Writes About George

Lots of people saw the posters. Soon the whole street knew about George. A reporter came to Katie and Mackenzie's house. First he asked their mom for permission. Then he wrote a story for the paper.

Saturday July 22   *The Scarborough Windows*
LOOKING FOR GEORGE
Daniel H. Staff Reporter

Two Scarborough children want to do something better than all the king's horses and all the king's men. They want to put something back together again.

This time it's not a broken egg. It's a little figure made out of plastic. His name is George.

On fireworks day, George's rocket went out of control. It exploded. George went to pieces. A leg and shoe fell back to the yard right away. The left arm and hand landed a few days later. Fisherman Jonah Trout found the other leg and shoe in the Rouge River.

Katie and Mackenzie are upset that the rest of the parts remain at large. The two children are especially worried about the head.

"I just wanted to give him a ride into space," said Mackenzie. "I gave George the best rocket ever."

"George has always found his way home before this," Katie said. "I hope to hear from the head soon."

The newspaper added a note at the bottom of the story:

George has red clothes and black hair. Anyone who finds a piece of George can send it to P.O. Box 7, care of the *Scarborough Windows* newspaper.

Katie and Mackenzie read the story.

"Too bad the paper didn't take my picture," said Katie.

"Too bad they didn't use one of my drawings," said Mackenzie.

"George is a pain," said Katie.

"George is a pest," said Mackenzie.

Katie cut out the newspaper story.

Mackenzie stuck it on the fridge.

George's Middle
Goes To Press

George's middle landed in a recycle bin outside a house. It landed in a can of beans. One night a bandit in a black mask stole the piece out of the can.

The bandit was a fat raccoon. Maybe the raccoon liked red plastic covered in bean juice. Maybe it thought George's middle was a big bean. Luckily it didn't think the middle was a meatball.

The next day the kids in the house went outside to play. One of the kids drew a hopscotch court on the driveway.

All the kids looked for a throwing piece. One kid found a loonie in his pocket. Two kids found stones. Another kid picked up George's middle. It was the best throwing piece. It stayed put.

At lunchtime the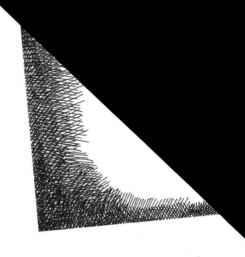

way. They even left t

The pickup driver c

truck right on top of

his door, he saw the l

That's what pickup dri

Then he saw Georg

said. "Somebody stuck

truck. There's even a story about it in the paper." He

picked the red piece up. He was a good pickup driver.

The pickup driver started his truck again. He drove

all the way down to the *Scarborough Windows* newspa-

per office. He threw the red plastic piece over to the

front door. George's plastic middle landed just right.

It stayed put.

Before he went home, the driver looked back a couple

of times. He wanted to make sure nobody was looking.

He didn't want people to think he was playing with toys.

"I'll never tell anyone I did that," he said out loud.

"They'll think I'm a fool."

George's Arm
Takes the Train

A plastic arm fell through the fireworks. It fell on top of a night train that rumbled through town. It was a right arm. It had a right hand.

The hand couldn't see the train, but it could sure feel the *clackety-clack*.

Every once in a while the train went faster. Then the wheels went *clatyclack*. When the train went the fastest, there was just a *clack*.

The arm and the hand tapped out the rhythm.

Clackety-clack, clackety-clack, clackety-clack,
Clatyclack, clatyclack, clatyclack,
Clack, clack,
Clackety-clack,

Clatyclack,

Clack, clack, clack!

The arm and the hand were a good team. An arm and a hand like that could lift weights. They could throw baseballs. Maybe they could wash windows.

Days came and went. The train ran between forests and lakes. It ran between wheat fields. A wind came up. It blew the arm and the hand right off the train.

Clink! Clinkety, clink, clink, clink!

The arm and the hand hit the track. On the last bounce the hand grabbed some lunch.

It was Hobo Bob's lunch.

Hobo Bob
Reads About George

Hobo Bob took out his lunch. It was a big onion sand-wich wrapped up in a piece of newspaper. While he ate his lunch, he spread the newspaper over the rocks and read the stories.

Hobo Bob always read the newspaper. He was a good reader. Sometimes the newspaper was a day old. Sometimes it was a week old. That didn't matter. It was news to him.

He saw the little plastic hand hooked on the edge of the paper. He picked up the hand. Then he saw the arm. Hobo Bob looked at them for a while. Then he put the hand and the arm in his pocket.

He ate his onion sandwich and read the paper. He read a story about a baby who won a million dollars. He read a story about a dog who could count to ten. He read the story about George.

Bob was a hobo, but he was still a gentleman. He wrapped up the arm and the hand in the newspaper and tied it with a piece of string. He wrote the address on the paper with the stub of an old pencil.

He wrote…

P.O. Box 7
Care of the Scarborough Windows newspaper
Scarborough

He gave the package to the woman who lived in a farmhouse along the track.

The next time she went to town, she mailed the package. She was a classy lady.

Too Many Parts
Pile Up

It was a busy day at the *Windows* office.

A reporter opened a package. "Here's another arm," he said. He wrinkled his nose. The package smelled like onions. He made a check mark on his list. "That's twenty-seven red arms," he said.

"Not another one," the editor said. "Tomorrow we're going to take that box over to those kids. We've got a paper to run."

They looked at the box in the corner of the office. It was piled with parts. Another reporter said, "That box is already too full. We need a bigger box."

A photographer walked in. He held up George's middle. "This was outside the front door," he said.

The editor was opening another letter. It was from Japan. A pair of black goggles fell out of the envelope.

Everyone groaned.

The editor pointed to the box full of parts. "At this rate," she said, "we're going to need a box big enough to hold a refrigerator."

Katie and Mackenzie Find More of George

Katie was looking out the window. A *Scarborough Windows* truck pulled up.

Two people carried a big box to the front porch. They left in a hurry.

Katie and Mackenzie pulled the box into the hall. It was filled with plastic pieces. There were lots of colors.

Katie shook her head.

"This is your fault," she said to her brother. "Your drawings weren't good enough."

"It's your fault," said Mackenzie. "Nobody can read your writing."

Katie fished in the box. "Yes they can," she said. "George's middle is in this box. His right arm is here too."

"Somebody must have seen my pictures," said Mackenzie.

Katie got George's left arm and his pair of legs from the kitchen shelf. She attached them to the body. Then she attached the right arm.

"Too bad there's no head," she said. "George is not much good without his head."

"He's not much good anyway," said Mackenzie.

Mackenzie looked through the box. He found a plastic body with big shoulders. "Here's a body with muscles," he said.

Katie took two legs out of the box. One leg was soft and fat. The other one wore blue tights. "Give me that body," she said to her brother. "These legs will fit."

Mackenzie looked in the box again. He picked out two arms. One arm had a hand with grabby fingers. The other arm had a tattoo. It didn't have a hand. It had a hook.

The arms fit too.

"Find a head," said Katie.

Mackenzie found a head with a long thin face and a snarly mouth. Who knows why the face snarled. Maybe it saw a bad guy. Maybe it was a bad guy. Maybe it had something stuck up its nose.

Mackenzie said, "We could stick this head on George's body."

"No way!" Katie said. "You can't use another head for George. Then it wouldn't be George. It would be somebody else."

She stuck the head on the body with the big muscles. It made a funny-looking guy. The head snarled worse than ever.

"Nobody wants a guy that looks like that," Mackenzie said. He took it apart and threw the pieces back in the box. Then he went to the door and scratched *Body* and *Right arm and hand* off the poster.

Now only the head was missing.

Katie and Mackenzie Make Two Guys and Two Dolls

Katie and Mackenzie spent the rest of the afternoon playing with the plastic parts. They looked through the newspaper box. They looked through the box under the door. Some of the parts didn't belong to play people. There was a cookie cutter and a little plastic house from a board game. But lots of the pieces fit together.

Katie and Mackenzie picked out some of the best ones. It was time to make some new figures.

Katie made a good-looking guy. She put the head with the snarl on a body with a long blue mackintosh and a white dress shirt. She added pink gloves and black-and-white shoes. "His name is Mr. Dab," she said.

Mackenzie made a guy too. He shoved a shaved head onto the body with the big abs and pecs. He added two arms with solid fists and two legs with boots. "The blue helmet will look good on this guy," said Mackenzie. "I'm going to call him Battle Ram."

Then they made a doll. She ended up mostly yellow. She had a smiley yellow head, a round yellow belly, purple legs with yellow shoes and stretchy yellow arms with white hands. They named her Yellow Melon.

After that there were only two pieces left on the floor. Katie stuck the two pieces together. "This makes another doll," she said.

Mackenzie looked at the doll. "She's got no clothes," he said.

"She needs to go shopping," said Katie.

It was time for dinner. Mackenzie put Mr. Dab, Battle Ram and Yellow Melon on the shelf in the kitchen. Mackenzie put most of George on the shelf too. The motorcycle was already there.

Katie put the second doll on the shelf. "If we find George's head, she can be his girlfriend," she said.

"George doesn't need a girlfriend," said Mackenzie.

George
Heads for Home

George woke up. It was dark and cold. All he could see were purple heads—purple heads with big bulgy eyes and tiny little hairs.

It started to get warm. The purple people began to talk. They sputtered and spattered.

George didn't understand a word they were saying. It was all nonsense to him. But he paid attention anyway. Maybe he could learn a new language.

Too bad the purple heads went back to sleep when it cooled down.

George looked around. Suddenly he saw a pair of giant lips. He saw a thick tongue and greedy teeth. The tongue wanted to suck on his eyeballs. The teeth wanted to grind his bones. A giant purple people eater was going to swallow him!

George put on his thinking cap. He was not going to be somebody's dessert. He took a deep breath. He took another and another. His head filled with air. His face stretched. It stretched as tight as a party balloon, as tight as a rope in a tug-of-war, tighter than last year's pants.

George blew his top!

Out! Out! George shot through space. He was headed for home! He was George the Brave, George the Steadfast. He would complete his mission.

He would get a makeover!

George
Gets Out of a Jam

Katie and Mackenzie went to the fun fair. First they went to the fish pond. Katie pulled up a blue fish. She won a bag of blueberry candied popcorn. Mackenzie pulled up a red fish. He won a bag of cherry sours.

They played beanbag toss in the gym. The prizes were stickers. Mackenzie chose a scratch-and-sniff sticker of a pickle. Katie chose a sticker of a fuzzy pig.

Next they went to the used-book sale. Katie bought a book about how to fix motorcycles. Mackenzie bought a comic about a superhero who could breathe underwater.

After that they went to the food stand. All the moms and dads had made good things to eat. Mackenzie bought a hot dog with cheese. Katie bought a chocolate chip muffin. The lemonade was free. They sat down at one of the tables to eat.

Pitouee!

The kid next to Mackenzie spat out his mouthful of blackberry pie. It landed on the table with a splatter.

"Eeeuuw!" said Mackenzie.

"Gross," said Katie.

"There was something in there," the kid said. "Something hard."

Mackenzie and Katie looked at the pie spit.

Katie said, "Do you see what I see?"

"George is there all right," said Mackenzie.

"Pick him up," said Katie.

"No way," Mackenzie said. "You pick him up."

One of the dads came over with a wet rag. Katie and Mackenzie both grabbed at the spit.

"Eeeuuw!" said the boy who spat out the pie.

"Eeeuuw!" said the other kids at the table.

Mackenzie shoved the piece into Katie's napkin.

Then the kids recognized George. Some of them had read the newspaper. Some of them had seen a poster.

"Hey," said the kid with the pie. "I found that head first. I should get a reward."

Katie looked at Mackenzie. Mackenzie stuck out his pickle sticker.

"Haven't you got anything better than that?" the kid asked.

So Mackenzie gave him the comic about the super-hero with gills in his nose.

"Sweet," said the kid. He already had another mouthful of pie.

At home, Katie put George back together again. She put him on the shelf with the guys and the dolls.

Mackenzie went to the front door and scratched out the word *Head* on the poster. He scribbled out the word *Reward* too.

George
Falls for the Doll

George woke up in one piece. He had his arms and his big strong hands. He had his legs and his shiny red shoes. His jumpsuit was as snug as ever. He was perfect!

Something flashed. A motorcycle was parked right in front of him. It had three wheels with chrome spokes and a black leather seat. A triker! George could not believe his big blue eyes.

George looked again. A girl was standing on the other side of the bike. George's eyes almost fell right out of his head. She was the most beautiful girl in the world. She was a babe!

George stood tall. He put his shoulders back and stuck out his chest. He looked straight ahead. A girl like that would go for a tall guy in a red jumpsuit and shiny red shoes.

He was George the Brave, George the Steadfast. He would get the bike. He would get the girl. He would be the Guy with the Bike and the Babe!

Katie and Mackenzie Have Fun

"What are you doing?" said Mackenzie.

"I'm making a dress," said Katie. "It's for the doll." She sewed two pieces of lime green cotton together. The dress had a hole for each arm and a hole for the head.

Katie slipped the dress over the doll. "It's a bit tight," she said.

Mackenzie looked at the doll. "What's the matter with her hair?" he said.

The doll's hair stood up in points. "I cut it," Katie said. "It's supposed to look like that." She started to color the tips of the hair with a turquoise marker.

Mackenzie took George and the motorbike down from the shelf. He put George on the seat. George's hands fit over the handle grips.

Next, Mackenzie got the goggles from the box of parts. He put them over George's eyes. "George is going for a ride," he said.

"Everybody can watch," Katie said. She took Mr. Dab, Battle Ram and Yellow Melon down from the shelf.

Katie and Mackenzie took George and the others outside. Katie sat three figures on the side of the driveway. She put George's girl on top of the bottle of window wash in their father's car. Who knows why she did that.

Mackenzie wound up the bike.

"Just a minute!" Katie said. She took off Battle Ram's helmet. She put it over George's head. "This time all of George will come back," she said.

Mackenzie let the bike go.

George
Rides the Triker

George was ready to ride! A crowd waited along the track.

The girl with the turquoise hair was all by herself in the big car. She was watching him!

George gripped the handlebars of his bike. He held his breath. He waited.

She blew him a kiss!

Whew!

A hot wind swept past George's face. He almost melted on the spot—just like his thumb.

Vrooooom!

The bike took off like a stick of dynamite. The engine roared. The wheels spun so fast they smoked. George leaned forward. He let the wind slick back the waves in his hair. His bike ate up the track.

A roadblock appeared! George leaned to the right. The bike swerved off the road. It hit the dirt. The tires tore up the field.

Ra-ta-ta-tat!

Sticks and stones rained down on George. Lucky he had his jumpsuit. Lucky he had his goggles and his helmet. He was no crash-test dummy. Safety came first!

George eased up on his speed. He wheeled the bike back to the blacktop. It rolled to a stop on the finish line.

The fans roared. They clapped. They cheered. They pounded each other on the back.

George held his breath. He waited. He waited for another kiss.

But the babe was gone.

Katie and Mackenzie, Oh-Oh!

Katie and Mackenzie waved goodbye to their dad. He backed the car out of the driveway. He had to go to the grocery store.

"Look," Mackenzie said, "George is back. He stopped on my shoelace."

"He always comes back," said Katie. "Wind him up some more."

Mackenzie wound up the wheels as tight as a top. "This bike is going to burn rubber," he said. He let the bike go.

It ripped down the drive.

"Oh-oh," said Mackenzie. "That bike is going way too fast."

"Oh-oh," said Katie. "George will get a speeding ticket."

They watched some more.

"George is gone," Katie said.

Mackenzie looked at Mr. Dab, Battle Ram and Yellow Melon. He looked at the empty driveway. "The girl is gone too," he said.

"She is not," said Katie. "She just went in the car to buy milk."

Bye-Bye!

George looked straight ahead. Where was his girl—his beautiful girl?

Suddenly he saw her turquoise hair in the car window. She was leaving him! Her lovely little arm waved in the air.

Bye-bye.

George's eyes got misty. Something stuck in his throat. His heart hurt.

George gathered his courage. He would not give up. He would go on. He was George the Brave, George the Steadfast.

Vrooooom!

He stepped on the gas.

He had a date with destiny!

Coming soon!

Part Three:
George, the Best of All

Will George make his dreams come true?

Will Katie and Mackenzie see him again?